Eve on the Lake

written and illustrated by
Todd Mikkelson

First published by AuthorHouse 11/30/05

ISBN: 1-4208-9469-2 (sc)

Library of Congress Control Number: 2005910244

Printed in the United States of America
Bloomington, Indiana

This book is printed on acid-free paper.

authorHOUSE

1663 LIBERTY DRIVE
BLOOMINGTON, INDIANA 47403
(800) 839-8640
www.authorhouse.com

Dedicated to Eve's grandparents
Hugo and Mary Ann Marty, LeRoy Mikkelson,
and especially Delores Mikkelson whom we so nearly lost

edited by Heidi Marty
photography by Todd Mikkelson, Heidi Marty, and Eve
Summer 2005

Eve lives with her mama and daddy in a little yellow house on the lake.

When she looks out her bedroom window, she sees her daddy's boat. Eve loves to go boating on the lake.

Eve asks, "Daddy, can we go out in the boat and see the buoys?" Her daddy answers, "Sure, little Eve, since you asked so nicely."

They go together to the kitchen and get the boat key.

Once they have the key, Eve and her daddy walk through the yard and out to the boat.

In the yard they pass by some flowers. "Hello, flowers!" says Eve.

Eve gets excited as they step onto the dock. "Hello, boat!" she shouts.

Once they're in the boat, Eve's daddy helps her put on her life jacket.

Her daddy unties the boat from the dock, starts the motor, and off they go.

After driving a short time Eve's daddy says, "There's a red one, Eve!"

Eve looks to the side of the boat and sees a red buoy. "Hello, buoy!" says Eve.

Eve begins to notice all the other things that can be found on the lake. First she sees a family of ducks. "Hello, ducks!" she says.

Then she sees some geese. "Hello, geese!" Eve says happily.

And then they come upon a seagull perched on a striped buoy. "Hello, seagull!"

Soon they see a bunch of big trees sticking out of the water. "What's that, daddy?" asks Eve. "That's an island," her daddy says. "Hello, island!" Eve shouts.

Then they see a heron standing on a rock. "Hello, heron!" says Eve.

Too quickly their boat ride comes to an end, and Eve and her daddy arrive back home.

As they walk up to the house, Eve's mama waves to them and says, "Come on, Eve, it's time to get ready for bed."

Eve's mama and daddy get her changed and her mama tucks her into her cozy bed.

They think she's fallen asleep, but then suddenly Eve opens her eyes and shouts "Daddy!" Her daddy is startled and asks, "What's wrong, little Eve?"

With a sweet little smile she asks, "Can we go out in the boat and see the buoys?"

"But baby, it's nighttime" her daddy replies. "Everything goes to sleep in the nighttime, just like you need to do. All the things we see on the lake are going to sleep now, just like you."

"The buoys are sleeping."

"The ducks are sleeping."

"The seagull is sleeping."

"The geese are sleeping."

"The island is sleeping."

"The heron is sleeping."

"Mama's flowers are sleeping."

"Even the boat is sleeping."

And when Eve's daddy finishes naming all the things that are sleeping, he sees that she has drifted off to sleep too. Sweet dreams, little Eve!

Printed in the United States
59923LVSX00048B